In the same series
At the Cinema
Football
Wakey-wakey

First published 2015 by order of the Tate Trustees
by Tate Publishing, a division of Tate Enterprises Ltd,
Millbank, London SW1P 4RG
www.tate.org.uk/publishing

Originally published in French as *Poka & Mine. Au fond du jardin*
Text and illustrations by Kitty Crowther
© l'école des loisirs, Paris 2007
This English edition © Tate Enterprises Ltd 2015
English translation by Ann Drummond in association with First Edition
Translations Ltd, Cambridge, UK © Tate Enterprises Ltd 2015

A catalogue record for this book is available from the British Library
ISBN 978-1-84976-245-8
Distributed in the United States and Canada by ABRAMS, New York
Library of Congress Control Number applied for

Printed in Italy by Grafiche AZ

Kitty Crowther

POKA & MIA

At the Bottom
of the Garden

TATE PUBLISHING

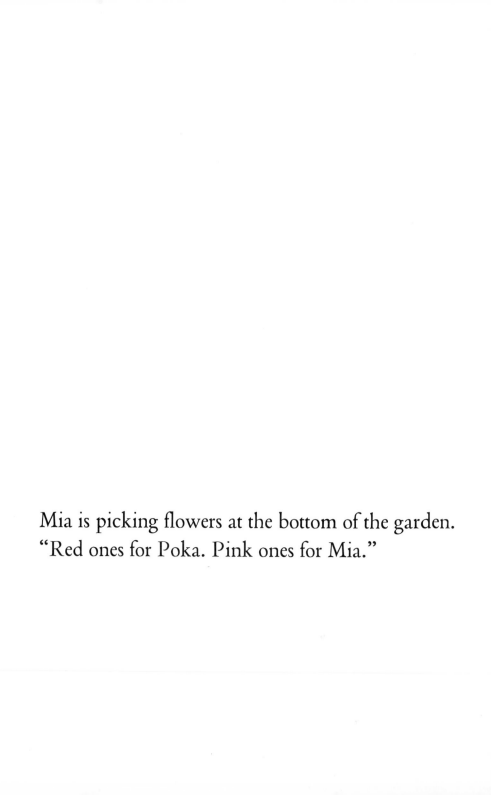

Mia is picking flowers at the bottom of the garden.
"Red ones for Poka. Pink ones for Mia."

Something moves behind her.
Someone is watching her. She is sure of it.
Mia hurries back to the house.

"Who on earth could be at the bottom of the garden?"
Before going back in to see Poka,
she looks over her shoulder one last time.

"Wonderful! Flowers for the table!"
declares Poka.
Then he looks at Mia and asks:
"Are you ok, Mia?"
"Yes, fine," she replies quietly.

It's getting dark outside.
Poka wonders what is going on
in Mia's little head.
"Are you sure you're ok?" Poka asks again.
"Fine, Poka, really," replies Mia.

It's time for bed.
"Good night, little Mia."
"Good night, Poka."

Mia can't get to sleep.
She gets up and looks out of the window.
There is a glimmer of light at the bottom of the garden.
Mia shivers.

The next day, after breakfast,
Poka says:
"Are you coming shopping with me?"
"No," Mia replies, "I'd rather stay here."

Mia wants to investigate.
Who is at the bottom of the garden?
She spots a strange ladder at the foot of the tree.

"Is anybody there?" she asks.
She discovers a small trapdoor.
Knock, knock. No reply.

Mia decides to go in.
What a strange house!

"Hello," says Mia.
"I knocked a few times."

All of a sudden, Mia finds herself a prisoner.
"Are you going to eat me?" she asks,
her voice shaking.
"You really think I'm going to eat meat?!"

The strange animal coughs.
"Are you sick?" asks Mia.
"I'll look after you. Let me go."

Quick as a flash, the strange animal sets her free.
"My name is Arto.
My throat hurts. I'm shivering."
"That's quite normal when you have a fever."

Mia takes Arto home with her, and puts him in the guest room.

"Here's a herbal tea and a scarf for you."

"Thanks, Mia," he says, in a hoarse voice.

"What a lovely scarf!"
"I knitted it myself."
"That's amazing! Will you teach me how to knit?"
"Of course,
but now you need to rest."

While Arto is sleeping,
Mia tells Poka the whole story.
He listens very carefully.

Later that day,
Mia goes to see her friend Arto.
"Poka agrees that you should rest.
Look, I've brought you a sweater."

"You're a spider,
so you'll need two extra sleeves.
Copy me."

"You've finished already!
That's amazing!"

"Look Poka, this is my friend Arto.
I've taught him how to knit."
"Hello, Mr Poka.
Do you have any more wool?"

After dinner,
they spend a great evening, knitting together.
"I'll never be cold again," says Arto.

The next day,
Arto goes back home, very happy indeed
and two days later, Poka and Mia
receive a gift-wrapped parcel.
"Bring on winter!" laughs Poka.